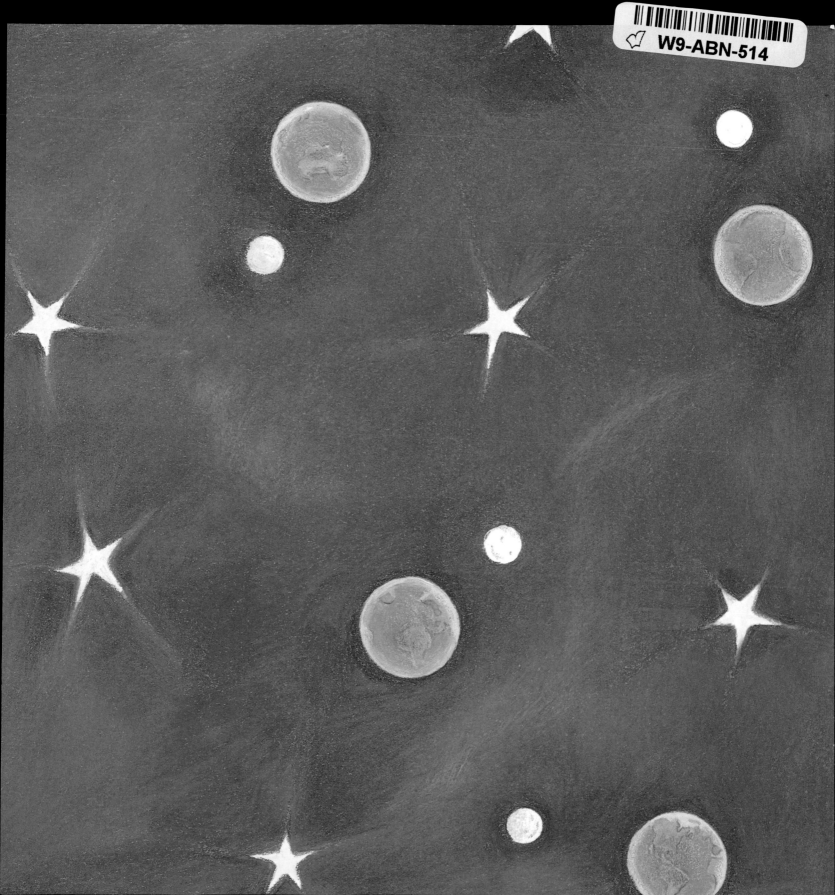

Goodnight, World

Andrea Lynn Beck

North Winds Press
An Imprint of Scholastic Canada Ltd.

It's bedtime here,
in my home on the sea.
We're snug in our bunks,
my brother and me.

I'm thinking of you,
wherever you are.
If we look up,
will we see the same star?

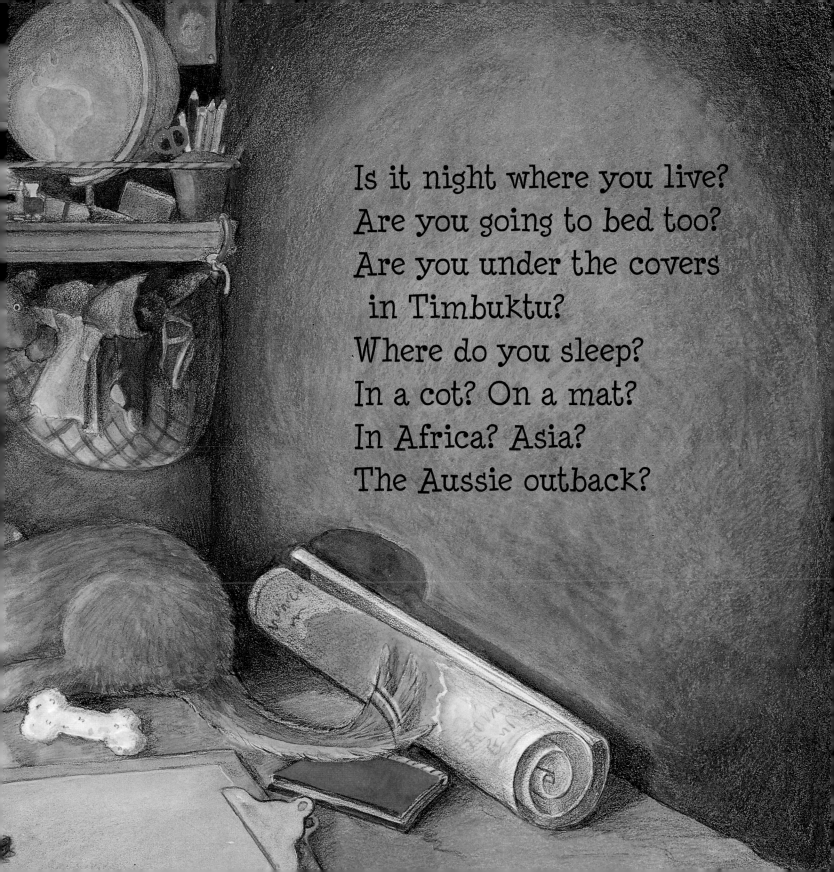

Is it night where you live?
Are you going to bed too?
Are you under the covers
 in Timbuktu?
Where do you sleep?
In a cot? On a mat?
In Africa? Asia?
The Aussie outback?

Are you in the Antarctic,
or Europe, perhaps?
North America?
South America?
Let's look at our maps!

I wonder about
the place you call home.

Is it inside a cave?
Or shaped like a dome?

Is your house made of brick?

Does your roof have a goat?

Maybe you live in a house that can float!

Do you sleep in a yurt?

Or a tree house high?

Perhaps you sleep way up in the sky!

Is your roof made of straw?
Are your walls made of mud?

Is your home up on stilts
in case of a flood?
Wherever you sleep,
wherever you are.
I'll think of you
when I look at that star.

Our world is so big,
 and sometimes so small.
It is our home,
 goodnight to us all.
Goodnight to me,
 goodnight to you.
Goodnight to us,
 and our world too.

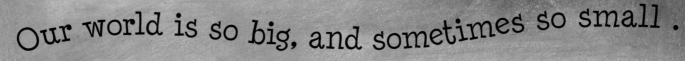

Our world is so *big*, and sometimes so small . . .

I once met a boy who lived aboard a sailboat in Grenada. He inspired this story. There are many families, and even whole villages of people, all over the world who live on the sea.

The domed houses were inspired by the beehive houses of Syria. Domed homes can be made from nearby materials, such as mud, sod and earth, or concrete, wood, steel, plastic and even snow!

The brick house in this story is made out of clay bricks that were baked in a giant oven called a kiln. Bricks stand up to weather well and can last over 100 years. They can be used for single homes, row houses and apartment buildings.

Sturdy yurts made of wood and felt are still built by nomads who follow their herds of sheep, goats and yaks across the steppes of Eurasia. Yurts are easily packed up and taken to the next grazing spot. Today, they can also be found in Mongolian cities.

I once visited a country market that had goats grazing on the roof. I wanted goats on MY roof! Grass roofs are still mostly found on homes in Scandinavia and Iceland, but they can be found elsewhere too, even on tall city buildings.

Houseboat homes are different from sailboat homes because houseboats usually stay in one place. Many waterfront cities have permanently moored houseboats in their harbours and canals. These floating homes are sometimes colourful and whimsical, like the houseboats in this book.

The tree house in this story is a magical place that a child might imagine. There are some unusual tree houses in the world where families do live, but most are treetop hotels for tourists or backyard playhouses for children.

Most cities have large buildings that are divided into small separate homes called apartments, flats, units or condominiums. These buildings allow many more people to live in a city than if each family had a separate house.

Mud homes are inexpensive and sturdy, and they stay cool under the sun! Walls of mud homes are made from earth, sand, clay or dung mixed with sticks and straw, all materials that are found nearby. Sometimes a whole village will help build the home.

I once stayed in a stilted home that had beautiful breezes blowing through because it was high above the ground. The stilts also kept the house safe from the flooding of the nearby river. It was a wooden home, much like the one in this picture.

It is our home, goodnight to us all.

There are many different kinds of wooden houses in the world. My house looks like this one!

Hi, I'm Andrea Lynn Beck. I wrote and illustrated *Goodnight, World*. When I was small, I would look up at the stars and wonder who else was staring at the sky at that very moment. Do you do that? I have been lucky to travel to many places in the world and it has taught me that no matter where we live or how different we seem, we are the same in the most important ways. We are a family and Earth is our precious home.

To Kathryn and John,
who follow their star.

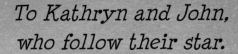

The illustrations for this book were created using pencil crayon
and paint on watercolour paper.

Library and Archives Canada Cataloguing in Publication

Beck, Andrea, 1956-, author, illustrator
Goodnight, world / Andrea Lynn Beck.

ISBN 978-1-4431-4865-8 (hardcover)

I. Title.

PS8553.E2948G67 2019   jC813'.54   C2018-906662-8

www.scholastic.ca

5 4 3 2 1   Printed in Malaysia 108   19 20 21 22 23